For Leah, who waited; M.I.B
For Sofia, Joakim and Lauren; H.D.

HarperCollins*Publishers*

No plain pets!

NORDS by MARC IAN BARASCH   piCTURES by HENRIk DRESCHER

It's Time for a PET,
I told MOM Last Night.
She RAISED up ONE Eyebrow,
Then said, "WELL, ALL Right."

But MOM, I went on,
I don't want one that's plain—
some dumb PUFF of FLUFF
with a paRakEET BRAIN.

Flying Fish don't JUST
BLOW BUBBLES and STARE
THEY FLAP ALL Their Fins
And SOAR OFF Through the air!

Our FREEZER'S
JUST PERFECT
FOR
Penguins galore
ONE ICE bath,
TWICE DAILY,
THEN **HOT** tea
AT FOUR.

A JUNGLE SNAKE HUGS YOU
FROM EVERY DIRECTION
IT'S JUST A SNAKE'S WAY
OF SHOWING AFFECTION.

DESPITE, WHAT YOU'RE THINKING
HE WON'T ask A LOT of US.

A GOAT WOULD CLEAN UP
AFTER ME EVERY DAY:
LEGO BLOCKS,
DIRTY SOCKS,
GREEN CLUMPS
OF
CLAY.

OR, WHAT ABOUT...
A THING THAT SINGS LULLABIES
UNDER THE BED
AND MOVES WITH SIX LEGS
STICKING OUT OF ITS HEAD,
THAT GOBBLES COLD CEREAL
RHUBARB AND RUBBER,
WHOSE ONE PART IS SKINNY
AND THE OTHER PART BLUBBER?
BUT MOM, THE MAIN THING
ISN'T REALLY WHAT KIND...

No Plain Pets!
Text copyright © 1991 by Marc Ian Barasch
Illustrations copyright © 1991 by Henrik Drescher
Printed in Mexico. All rights reserved.

Library of Congress Cataloging-in-Publication Data
Barasch, Marc.
   No plain pets! / words by Marc Ian Barasch ; pictures by Henrik Drescher.
      p.   cm.
   Summary: A child enumerates the many exotic pets there are from which to choose,
from big black gorilla to an imaginary thing with six legs sticking out of its head.
   ISBN 0-06-022472-X. — ISBN 0-06-022473-8 (lib. bdg.)
   ISBN 0-06-443375-7 (pbk.)
   [1. Pets — Fiction 2. Animals — Fiction 3. Stories in rhyme.]
I. Drescher, Henrik, ill. II. Title.
PZ8.3.B23434No   1991   90-22518
[E]—dc20   CIP
                                                                AC